How the W̶h̶a̶l̶e̶ got his Throat

MILES KELLY

Once upon a time
there was a whale, and he ate fish.

He ate the
starfish

and the
garfish

and the
crab

and the dab

and the
plaice

and the **dace**

and the really truly twirly-whirly eel.

He ate all the fish he could find in all the sea.

One day the whale said,
"I'm hungry."

There was now only
one small fish left in all the
sea and he said, "Noble and
generous whale, have you
ever tasted man?"

"No," said the whale. "What is it like?"
"Nice," said the fish. "Nice but nubbly."

Splash!

"Then fetch me some," boomed the whale.

"One at a time is enough," said the clever fish. And he told the whale where he could find a man.

So the whale SWAM and SWAM
as fast as he could swim.

At last, in the middle of the sea,
he came to a raft.

On the raft was a solitary
shipwrecked sailor,
trailing his toes in the water.

He wore blue trousers
held up with braces and he
carried a knife, and they
were the only things he
had left in the world.

The whale opened his mouth
back and **back** and **back**
till it nearly touched his tail,
and he swallowed the
sailor in his blue
trousers and braces,
and his raft, and
his knife.

Gulp!

He swallowed them all down into his
warm, dark, inside cupboards.
Then he smacked his lips, and turned round
three times on his tail.

But as soon as the sailor found
himself inside the whale's warm,
dark, inside cupboards...

and he stumped
and he jumped

he thumped
and he bumped

and he hit
and he bit

and he banged
and he clanged

and he hopped
and he dropped

and he
prowled
and he
howled

and he danced hornpipes
where he shouldn't.

The whale felt most unhappy indeed.
So he said to the clever little fish,

"This man is very nubbly,
and he is making me hiccup.
What shall I do?"

Hic!

"Tell him to come
out," said the fish.

So the whale called down his own throat to the sailor, "Come out and behave yourself. I've got hiccups."

"No!" said the sailor. "Take me home, and I'll think about it." And he began to dance more than ever.

"You had better take him home," said the clever little fish.

So the whale SWAM and SWAM and SWAM, with both flippers and his tail – as hard as he could, with his hiccups.

Hiccup!

But while the whale was swimming, the sailor took his **knife** and cut up his **raft** to make a little square grating all running criss-cross.

He tied it firm with his **braces**.

And he wedged that grating good
and tight into the whale's throat,
and there it stuck!

At last the whale saw the
shore and he rushed halfway up
the beach, and opened his mouth
wide and wide and wide, and said,

"We're at your stop!"

"Time to go!"

The sailor stepped out on the beach, and went home, where he married and lived happily ever after.

But before he went, he waved goodbye to the whale and sang,

"By means of a grating I've stopped your 'ating."

The clever little fish went and hid himself in the mud just under the door of the equator.

"Shhhhh!"

He was afraid that the whale might be angry with him.

And the whale didn't find him – not until he got out of his temper, and then they were good friends again.

From that day on, the grating in the whale's throat – which he could not cough up nor swallow down – stopped him eating anything except very, VERY small fish.

The starfish and the
garfish and the crab
and the dab and all the
others were most
relieved.

And that is the reason why whales
today never eat sailors -
or little boys or girls.